Along the Beach

Acknowledgments
Executive Editor: Diane Sharpe
Supervising Editor: Stephanie Muller
Design Manager: Sharon Golden
Page Design: Simon Balley Design Associates
Photography: Biofotos: pages 6, 8, 13, 18; Bruce Coleman: pages 20-21; Image Bank: cover (all); Oxford Scientific Films: pages 9, 17, 22, 24-25, 27.

ISBN 0-8114-3792-2

Copyright © 1995 Steck-Vaughn Company.

All rights reserved. No part of the material protected by this copyright may be reproduced or utilized in any form or by any means, electronic or mechanical, including photocopying, recording, or by any information storage and retrieval system, without permission in writing from the copyright owner. Requests for permission to make copies of any part of the work should be mailed to: Copyright Permissions, Steck-Vaughn Company, P.O. Box 26015, Austin, TX 78755.
Printed in the United States of America.
British edition Copyright © 1994 Evans Brothers.

1 2 3 4 5 6 7 8 9 00 PO 00 99 98 97 96 95 94

Along the Beach

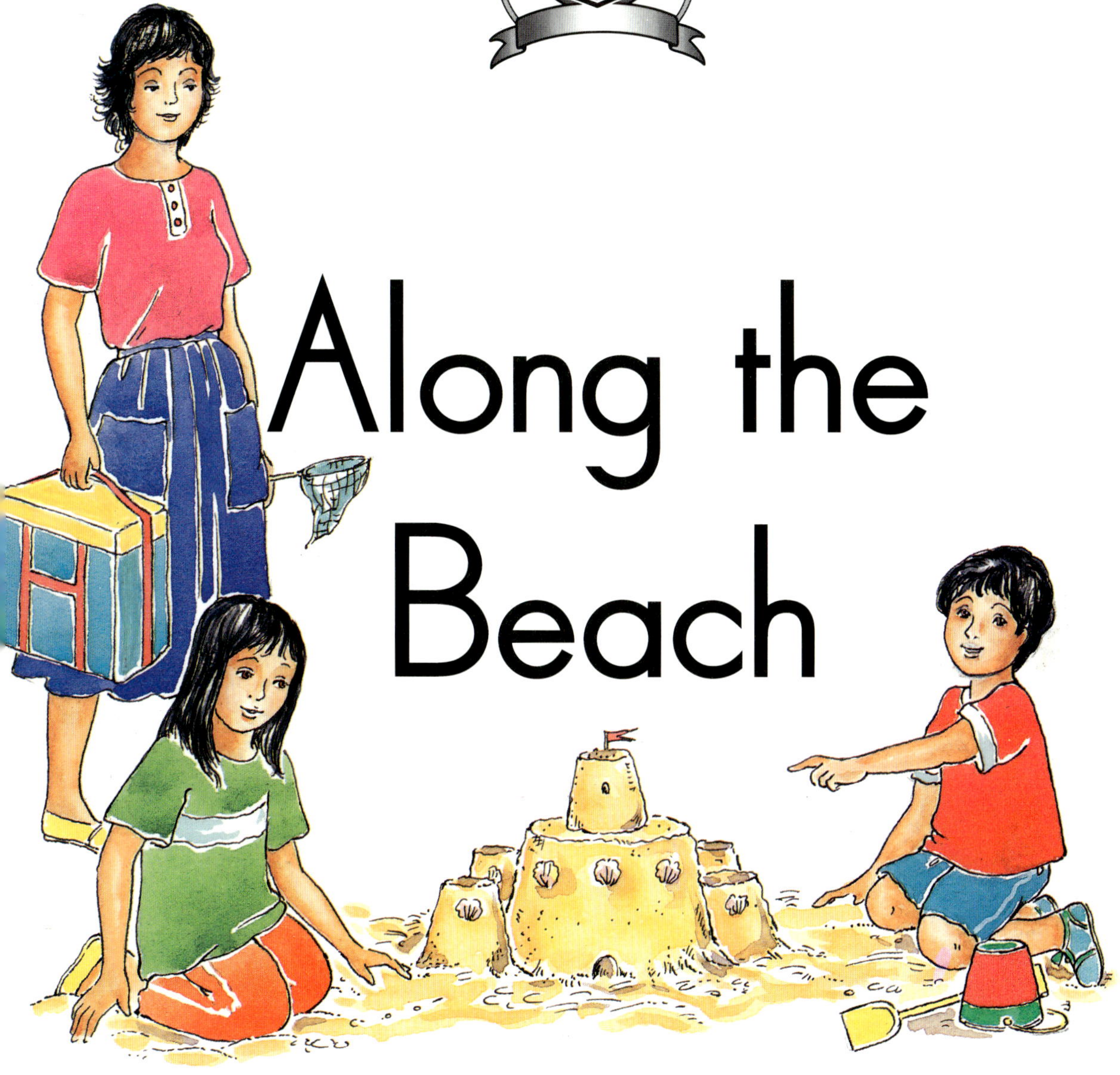

Mike Jackson

Illustrated by
Kareen Taylerson

Sand that is farther from the ocean is dry because the water does not reach it.

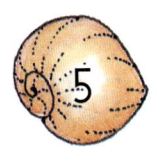

The ocean tide comes in and goes out twice each day. When the tide comes in, it is called high tide. This line shows us how far the water comes in at high tide.

They are the shells of small ocean animals.

When the animal inside the shell dies, waves wash the empty shell up on the beach.

Trash that is dumped in the ocean is washed up on the beach by the waves.

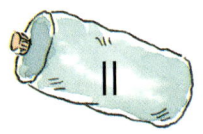

The wooden walls are called sea walls. They stop the sand from being pushed along the beach by wind and waves.

A red flag tells us that it is not safe to go swimming.

When it is not safe to swim, the lifeguard puts up a red flag. When it is safe, he puts up a green flag.

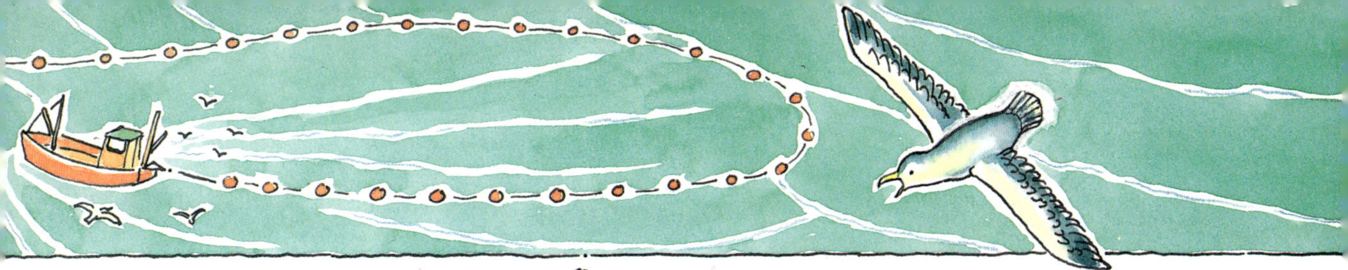

"I can see some fish in these boxes."

Fishers dock their boats in the harbor. A wall protects the boats in the harbor from big waves.

The fisher puts some bait inside the pot
and then lowers it into deep water.
The lobster can climb in to eat the bait,
but it cannot get out again.

When the tide goes out, it is called low tide. This muddy area shows us how far the water goes out at low tide.

That bird is called a sea gull.

Sea gulls search among the tide pools for crab and shrimp to eat.

All the pebbles are smooth, too. This one looks like an egg!

The movement of the waves rubs pebbles and glass against the sand. This wears them smooth after a long time.

The flashing light in the lighthouse warns ships in the ocean about dangerous rocks and sandbars.

The tide covers the sand twice a day, bringing in new shells and pebbles.
So there are different things to find on the beach every day.

Below are some things that can be seen on the beach. How many can you name? The answers are on the last page, but don't look until you've tried naming everything.

Index

Boats **16-17, 30**

Fish **17, 31**
Fisher **17, 19**
Flags **14-15, 30**

Harbor **17**
High tide **7, 28-29, 30**

Lifeguard **15**
Lighthouse **26-27, 31**
Lobster pots **18-19, 31**
Low tide **20-21**

Nets **16**

Ocean **5, 7, 11, 24, 29**

Pebbles **6, 24-25, 29**

Sand **4-5, 6, 12-13, 25, 29**
Sandbars **27**
Sand castle **4-5, 28-29**
Sea gull **22-23, 30**
Seashore **4**
Sea walls **12-13, 31**
Seaweed **6**
Shells **8-9, 29, 31**
Swimming **14-15**

Tide pools **22-23**
Trash **10-11**

Waves **9, 11, 13, 17, 25**

Answers: 1. Red flag 2. High-tide mark 3. Fishing boat 4. Sea gull
5. Lighthouse 6. Sea wall 7. Fish 8. Lobster pot 9. Shells